FORELAND
POINT

LYNTON • LYNMOUTH

EAST LYN
RIVER

• YENWORTHY FARM
• PARSONAGE FARM

• MANOR FARM

BAGWORTHY   OARE
WATER

DUNSTER →

DOONE
VALLEY

■ PLOVERS
BARROW
FARM

EXMOOR

Lorna Doone *is such a good story that in the century or so since it was written it has become part of West Country legend. There is even a valley which is pointed out as 'Doone Valley', the home of the Doone outlaws!*

First edition

LORNA DOONE

by R D Blackmore

retold by Joan Collins

illustrated by Frank Humphris

Ladybird Books Loughborough

The End of Schooldays

My name is John Ridd. I was born and brought up in the West Country, on Plovers' Barrow Farm, in Exmoor, when King Charles II was on the English throne.

My father was a well respected farmer in the parish of Oare. He wanted me to be educated, so he sent me to Blundell's School, in Tiverton. But I was taken away when I was twelve years old, on my birthday, 29th November 1673.

I had spent all my pocket money on sweets for my friends, and we were leaning over the gate, scuffling with each other. A red-faced man came round the corner on a horse, leading a pony. He called out to the boys, 'Please, young masters, can 'ee tell me where our Jan Ridd be?'

'Here he be, your Jan Ridd!' answered a sharp little boy, making fun of his country way of talking.

'Let me see him, then!' says John Fry. He was one of my father's men.

5

'Oh, John!' I cried. 'Why have you come over the moors in this cruel cold weather, with my pony? The holidays don't begin till Wednesday fortnight!'

John Fry leaned forward in the saddle and turned his eyes away from me. Then he made a noise in his throat, like a snail crawling up a window-pane.

'We know that, well enough, master Jan. Your mother have kept all the apples stored, and old Betty have made your favourite black puddings – all for thee, lad. Every bit of it, now, for thee.'

He stopped and that frightened me.

'And Father – how is Father? John, is Father up in town? He always used to come for me himself.'

'Your father'll be waiting at the crooked post up by the shepherd's hut. He couldn't leave home on account of getting ready the Christmas bacon and cider.'

He looked at the horse's ears as he said it, and I knew it was a lie. My heart felt like a lump of lead. I was afraid to ask any more questions. I did not even stroke my pony Peggy's nose, though she came snuffling up to my fingers.

The Doones Ride By

It was a long way from Tiverton to the village of Oare and the road was full of holes, muddy and rocky. It was noon before we got to Dulverton, where we had to stop to rest the horses.

John Fry strode into the White Horse Inn, and shouted, as loud as if he were calling sheep on Exmoor, 'Hot mutton pasties for two travellers, in five minutes! Dish 'em up in the tin with the gravy!'
(It was worth waiting for, though it took longer than five minutes. That was fifty years ago, and I can still taste that gravy!)

I went out to the pump to wash my face. A lady's maid, very fine and foreign, came out to fetch a glass of water for her mistress. She teased me about my blue eyes, and called me her 'leetle boy', asking me to pump the water for her.

We saw her again later on the road, in a great lumbering coach, going to Watchet.

She had a beautiful little dark-haired girl with her, richly dressed, with soft brown eyes. A fine lady, with a lovely little boy on her lap, smiled sweetly at me and my pony, as they went past.

The coach took the other road, and we went on towards Oare. The journey got worse and worse as time went on. Fog came down thick over the moors. All we could see was our horses' heads jogging, and hear the splash of their hooves in the wet.

I could see John Fry's Sunday hat bobbing up and down in front of me. He was almost asleep in the saddle, with one shoulder hunched up. Suddenly he came awake.

'Mercy on us! Where be we now? Have we passed the old ash tree, John?'

I had not seen it. We listened, and then there was a low, mournful creaking sound, repeated three times. I knew it was made by the chains on the gibbet at the crossroads, where they hanged robbers.

'It be Red John Hannaford from the other side of the moor, who come over to steal our sheep!' said John Fry. 'Bless him for creaking so!'

For now we knew where we were, near the Doone track, two miles from Dunkery Beacon, the highest place on Exmoor.

'If it happens the Doones be about tonight, we must crawl on our bellies, boy!'

I knew what that meant – those bloodthirsty Doones of Bagworthy, the terror of all Devon and Somerset, outlaws, traitors, and murderers!

My legs began to tremble on Peggy's sides, as I heard the dead robber creaking in his chains behind us, and thought of the live ones in front.

Then we heard them! Horses' hooves on the splashy ground. Grunts of weary men. The noise of stirrups and clash of iron. The blowing from horses' hairy nostrils.

We slipped off our horses and lay flat in the heather, looking down on the riders below. With any luck, the Doones would think our horses were forest ponies.

Just as the first horseman passed, the fog lifted, and a strong red light shone in the sky. It was Dunkery Beacon, lighted to show the Doones the way home. It was a wild sight, flame and smoke streaming up, twisting, into the sky.

In the rocky glen below, the red glow showed up the horsemen. Heavy men, huge and reckless, carrying guns and dressed in leather, with iron breast plates. They went along like clouds in a red sunset.

Some had carcases of sheep slung behind them, others had deer, and one had a child flung across his saddle-bow, dead or alive I could not tell. But I caught a glimpse of dark hair and a bright dress, glittering with jewels.

I forgot the danger, and shouted down to them in anger. But they thought I was a moorland pixie, and laughed and rode on.

My father never came to meet us at the shepherd's hut, or the crooked post, or even at home.

But my mother and sisters came out, weeping. The Doones had killed my father on his way back from market. The other farmers with him had given up their money without a struggle. But my father stood up to the Doones. His horse came home without him, and next day his body was found on the moors.

The Doone Valley

My father was buried and so my mother was left a widow, with three fatherless children to bring up. In her grief and anger, she put a brown hood on her head, a black shawl round her shoulders, and, without a word to anybody, set off for the Doone Gate.

This was not really a gate, but the entrance to a dark tunnel. When she came out of it, she stood at the end of a deep green valley, a perfect oval, carved out of the mountains. Tall cliffs of rock surrounded it on all sides, and a little river ran down the middle.

There were fourteen rough houses, built of stone. One bigger one, at the end, belonged to the captain of the Doones.

It all looked very peaceful and innocent, but this was where the murderers lived.

My mother was trembling. She was only a farmer's wife, and the Doones were people of high birth. But she thought of her dead husband, and went on to speak to the captain.

A tall, white-haired old man, Sir Ensor Doone, came up to meet her, with a billhook in his hand, and hedging gloves on.

But he was no common man, she could tell from his voice and manner. She burst into tears as she told him what had happened to her husband.

Sir Ensor frowned. 'This is a serious matter, madam! Send Counsellor to me!' he commanded.

Counsellor Doone was a square-built man of enormous strength. He had a long grey beard and great eyebrows, overhanging his face like ivy on an oak. Sir Ensor told him what my mother had said.

Counsellor was unmoved by the sad tale. He said John Ridd had attacked the Doones first, and tried to rob them. Carver, Counsellor's son, had fired the fatal shot, only meaning to scare the robber away.

My mother was so amazed at this lying tale, she could say nothing. Sir Ensor even suggested John Ridd had been drunk!

As she stumbled away, drying her tears, someone came after her with a heavy bag of money.

'Captain sends you this,' he whispered. 'Take it to the little ones!'

But my mother let it fall as if it had stung her. She did not want the Doones' pity, nor their gold.

The Doones were a family of noble birth, who had lost their Scottish estates in a quarrel with their kinsman, the Earl of Lorne. Sir Ensor had offended Charles I and escaped justice to live in this remote valley, with his family. They raided the farms and villages for cattle and crops, and stole the farmers' daughters for wives.

They were all huge men. It was said that when they were twenty years old, each one had to stand barefoot in the great door-frame of Sir Ensor's house. If he did not fill it out, he was sent away from the valley. By the time I was twenty, I could have carried that door-frame away on my shoulders! People called me 'girt Jan Ridd', because I grew to be so big and tall. But that was some years ahead.

The Bagworthy Water

I was only fourteen when my next adventure with the Doones came. I had set out one cold February morning to catch fish from the brook for my mother's supper.

I slung my shoes round my neck and rolled up my knee-breeches, going barefoot in the icy water. I had a three-pronged fork, to spear the grey-spotted, transparent fish, as they darted among the pebbles or flipped into the shelter of the rocks.

I had gone about two miles upstream and stopped to eat some brown bread and cold bacon. My legs were so cold I had to scrub them with stinging nettles to get some warmth back into them.

Then I came upon another stream, running into our brook. It was wider and stronger, and came down from the Doone valley. This was the Bagworthy ('Badgery') Water, and even grown men were afraid to go up it.

But I had not caught enough fish, so I went on, under the overhanging branches, in and out of the deep dark pools by the bank. It was very silent, broken only by the cry of a startled bird.

Then I came upon a gap in the bushes, and a great black whirlpool, with foaming froth round its edges.

A steep waterfall came roaring down into it from high up in the steep cliffs above. It slid down, smooth as glass. There was only a narrow ledge on each side, like a staircase with no rails. I wanted to know what was at the top of it.

I started to climb up the side, and was nearly carried away by the rush of green water. Luckily, my fork stuck in a crack of the rock, and saved me.

Half drowned, I scrambled on. It was slimy underfoot, but I struggled to the top of the cliff, and toppled over it, tired out, into fresh air and sunshine.

*   *   *

A Boy and a Girl

When I came to myself, a little girl was kneeling at my side, rubbing my forehead with a handkerchief.

She looked down at me with great big dark eyes. I sat up and stared at her.

'What is your name and how did you come here, and what are these wet things in this big bag?' she asked.

'They are fish for my mother's supper, but you can have some if you like.'

'No shoes and stockings! Are you a poor boy?'

'No!' I said, rather annoyed. 'We are rich enough to buy this meadow! And I have got shoes and stockings. Look, here they are.

My name's John Ridd. What's yours?'

'Lorna Doone,' she answered timidly. 'I thought you'd know that.' She looked ashamed and began to cry.

'Don't cry, Lorna,' I said. 'I'm sure you never did anyone any harm!'

She was only eight years old, and I felt so sorry for her that I gave her a kiss. She looked rather offended, and wiped her lips. Then she said, 'Why did you come here? Don't you know they'd kill us if they find you with me?'

'Why?'

'Because you have found the way up! I do like you, John Ridd, but please go away! Come back another day!'

I promised I would one day, soon.

Just then, there was a shout down the valley. Lorna looked frightened. We crept into the bushes, as a dozen fierce men rode into the clearing, calling out 'Queenie! Queenie! Where's our little queen gone?'

Lorna crept out and lay on the grass, pretending to be asleep. I slipped back into the water, keeping my head just out of it, so that I could breathe.

The great rough men rode round and saw
Lorna. One picked her up and put her on his
saddle and marched away, with her purple
velvet skirt ruffling out under his black
beard. Lorna turned and waved to me, riding
beside the largest and fiercest ruffian.

Somehow, I got back down the waterfall,
the cold and greedy water lapping after me,
like a black dog.

Time passes at Plovers' Barrow Farm

Life went on at the farm and I forgot about Lorna. I tried to take my father's place as I grew up, and looked after my mother and sisters.

Annie was everybody's favourite, gentle and pretty, with pink cheeks and blue eyes. She was a good little cook. Lizzie spent all her time reading. Our housekeeper, old Betty Muxworthy, who had been father's nurse, kept us all in order.

We had a cousin, Tom Faggus, who was a highwayman! He was my hero.

One day, when the farmyard was flooded, our old drake was caught on a hurdle in the middle of the water, squawking his head off.

Tom Faggus rode up on his dainty mare, Winnie, into the rushing water and rescued the drake, who quacked his thanks. The sure-footed strawberry mare knew every word Tom said, and had saved his life more than once.

'Pretend to hit me,' said Tom, 'and see what she will do!'

I raised my hand, and Winnie caught me by the waistband and lifted me in the air.

She would have thrown me down and trampled on me, but Tom stopped her.

'Would any of your animals do that for you?' asked Tom. 'Winnie, you witch, we shall die together!'

Tom had never robbed a poor man or insulted a woman, and he had never shed anyone's blood. All good people liked him as much as they hated the Doones, for he gave money to the church, and to poor people.

Another visitor was my Uncle Ben Huckaback, my mother's brother. He was the victim of one of the Doones' heartless pranks.

They robbed him one foggy New Year's Eve, tied him face down on his pony and sent it wandering off over the moors. I found him, and later took him up into the hills to spy out the Doone Valley.

It was then I saw a little opening in the cliffs, no bigger than a rabbit hole, and a tiny white figure flit across it. I remembered my boyhood promise to go back one day to see Lorna Doone.

I resolved to keep it, for now I was a man of twenty one, and grown to be a match for any of the Doones.

The Return to the Waterfall

It was seven years since I had first climbed the Bagworthy Water. The stream, which had been up to my knees, only reached my ankles now. But the great black whirlpool and the rocky slide were still forbidding. I climbed with some labour to the top.

There I saw a lovely sight. Lorna was coming along the side of the stream among the primroses. A wreath of white violets was in her dark hair, and the setting sun cast its light behind her.

When she saw me, she turned to run away, but I just said, 'Lorna Doone!'

Then she remembered the barefoot boy she had saved from the Doones, and spoke to me kindly. I promised to come back, and bring her eggs from our farmyard. I was too shy to say more, or to stay longer. But I wanted very badly to see her again, Doones or no Doones.

So, in the spring, when the frost had gone and the lambs were at play in the daisies, I climbed the waterfall again.

Lorna was so frightened for my safety, she hid me in her secret bower in the cleft

of a rock. The entrance was hidden by a screen of ivy, and the cave inside was like a little room, with a carpet of soft grass, moss and wild flowers.

I laid out the eggs I had brought her on the moss. She shed a tear or two, for she said no one had ever been so kind to her before, in all her sixteen years.

Then she told me her story. The Doones called her their princess, because her dead father had been the eldest son of Sir Ensor, and so she was heiress to the little kingdom. Her grandfather was very old and strict, and she was afraid of Counsellor, her uncle.

She ought to have been happy in that pleasant valley, but the Doones were violent and brutal. There was no one to teach her what was right and what was wrong.

Worst of all, she was supposed to be going to marry Carver Doone when she was old enough. Her only friend was a little Cornish girl called Gwennie Carfax, who had been found wandering on the moors.

Lorna was so afraid the Doones would find me that I promised not to come again till she gave me a signal. But I was determined somehow to rescue her from their clutches.

Trouble in the West Country

When I returned home, I was called to London. Jeremy Stickles, the king's messenger, came to fetch me, at the bidding of Charles II. There was rebellion in the West Country. Judge Jefferies had been put in charge of finding out who were the king's enemies. He questioned me, but I knew nothing. All my friends were loyal, true subjects.

I told him about the law-breaking Doones, and put in a good word for Tom Faggus. (Tom was seeking the king's pardon, so that he could give up being a highwayman, and marry my sister Annie.)

The judge took a liking to me, but decided I was too honest to make a good spy. So I was allowed to go home. Almost a year had passed, and I was very worried about Lorna, left alone in the Doone Valley.

I went straight to the hilltop from which I could see Lorna's signal: a black cloth on a white stone. I went straight up to her.

'Where have you been?' she cried. 'I am in such trouble.'

The young Doones had been quarrelling about who should marry her, and had been

fighting each other. Sir Ensor and Counsellor wanted her to promise to marry Carver, to settle the matter. She was only seventeen and he was thirty five.

I had brought her a ring from London, a sapphire set in pearls. I told her how much I loved her and begged her to marry me.

'Oh, John, I like you very much,' she said, 'but I don't love you yet. Keep your ring a little while longer.' But she smiled so sweetly, it gave me hope that she might grow fond of me.

I did not see Lorna again for two months.

Meanwhile, there were rumours of secret meetings on the moors at night and stories of hidden weapons. Jeremy Stickles came down to spy out the land and brought troops with him. He warned me to keep on the right side of the law, on the king's side, against the rebels who supported the Duke of Monmouth.

Then at last Lorna sent for me. She told me she loved me, too, and would keep my ring. She gave me one in exchange – a heavy old gold thing, which had hung on the front of a glass necklace she had had as a child.

I went home a happy man. But the next time I climbed the waterfall, there was no sign of Lorna anywhere!

Lorna in Danger

I decided the only way to find out what had happened was to get into the valley from the other end. I had to risk it.

It was a long climb round the hills. I could not take a horse or show myself against the skyline in the moonlight.

When I reached the tunnel, I was lucky. Two sentries were squabbling over a game of cards, and one of them knocked over the lantern. I was able to slip by in the darkness.

I kept in the shadow of the houses till I came to the biggest one which I thought must be Sir Ensor's. There was a light in the window. I whispered Lorna's name, and, after a while, she came to the lattice window.

'You must be mad, John!' she exclaimed in fright.

'What has happened?' I asked.

'My poor grandfather is very ill, and Counsellor and Carver are in charge. I dare not leave the house for fear they seize me,' she replied.

Little Gwennie came to the window, too. 'He be bigger than any Doone!' she marvelled. 'Now missie, you go on courting, and I'll keep watch outside!'

Lorna and I fixed on a signal.

'You know the tree on the cliff that has seven rooks' nests in it?' she said. 'Gwennie can climb it, so if one day you see only six, you will know I am in trouble.'

One day I looked up at the tree, and there were only six nests. I started off for the valley at once. But, on my way, the short form of Gwennie Carfax came trotting out of the bushes to meet me.

'Old man be dying,' she said, 'and mistress have told him all about thee. He wants to see thee.'

We set off for the valley and went straight to Sir Ensor's house. Nobody stood in our way.

Two Fools Together

Gwennie led me into a cold, dark room, where two candles were burning. There was a white-haired old man with a stern, fine face, but the mark of death was on it. He was not in bed, but sitting proudly, bolt upright, with a red cloak over him. Only his great black eyes seemed alive as he stared angrily at me.

'Ah,' he said in a hollow voice, 'are you that great John Ridd?'

'John Ridd is my name, your honour.'

'And have you the sense to know what you are doing?'

'Yes, I know right well I have set my eyes far above my rank in wanting to marry Lorna.'

'Are you ignorant that Lorna Doone is born of one of the oldest families in Europe? And your own low descent from the Ridds of Oare?'

'Sir,' I answered, 'the Ridds of Oare have been honest men twice as long as the Doones have been rogues.'

The old man told me that the marriage was impossible, and sent me to fetch Lorna. I found her crying by a little window, so I put my arm round her and took her to her grandfather. She leaned her head on my waistcoat. I feared nothing when she was by my side.

Sir Ensor looked astonished. No one had ever defied him before. 'Ye two fools!' he said with contempt. 'Ye two fools!'

'Perhaps we are not such fools as we look!' I answered. 'But if we are, we shall be happy as long as we are two fools together.'

'Well, John,' said the old man, 'thou art not altogether the clumsy clod I took thee for!'

Sir Ensor leaned back on his brown chair rail. He coughed a little, and sighed. Perhaps he was remembering his own youth all those years ago.

'Fools you are; be fools for ever,' he said at last. 'That is the best I can wish you.' And his white hair fell like a shroud round his face.

I could not tell from that if he agreed to our marrying or not. But he seemed happy to have us both by his bedside.

Before he died, he fished under his pillow with his claw-like hand, and brought out Lorna's old glass necklace. She gave it to me for safe keeping.

Before Sir Ensor was buried, the greatest frost of the century set in. Strong men had to dig his grave with pick-axes. The sky was dark and heavy, and no one, except Lorna, shed a tear for Sir Ensor Doone.

The Great Winter

That year, before I could rescue Lorna from the Doone valley, winter set in.

One morning, I woke to find all the earth was flat with snow and the air thick with it. I made my way with difficulty to John Fry's cottage. We set out with pitchforks, shovels, ropes and Watch, our sheepdog, to the great meadow, where our sheep were.

And, lo and behold, there was no flock at all! Not a sheep to be seen anywhere, only a vast white sheet. In one corner of the field, the snow had drifted in a great white billow, as high as a barn.

There we heard a faint 'ma-a-ah' and dug away. The sheep were packed as closely under the snow as if they were in a great pie. Their warm breath had made a sort of arched room for them, lined with dirty yellow snow.

'However shall us get 'em home?' asked John Fry, for we could not drive them through the snow drifts.

'Good dog, Watch, keep them in!' I called
out. Then I took the two heaviest, one under
each arm, and carried them up to the
farmyard. I fastened them in the sheep pen,
and went back for two more. Sixty six
sheep I took home that way, all by myself.
Folk still talk about it on Exmoor, but
nobody but me knows what heavy work it
was, in all that snow and wind.

Over the Snow

At last some good came of my sister Lizzie's reading. She told me excitedly of a way she'd read about to walk over the snow. She showed me pictures of snow shoes and sledges used in the Arctic.

I made myself a pair of strong light snow shoes, with frames of ash wood, woven with willow twig, and covered with soft leather. The girls laughed at my clumsy efforts to walk on them. But at last with practice I managed, though it made my ankles sore and stiff.

You may guess that I set out for Doone Valley as soon as I could. It was snowed under, and looked like a great white pudding basin. When Gwennie opened the door at my signal, she gasped, 'Us be shut in here and starving! I wish thou wert good to eat, young man! I could manage most of thee.'

Counsellor Doone had shut his niece up without any food, till she agreed to marry Carver.

By good fortune I had brought one of Annie's golden brown mince tarts, and I divided it up between the two girls. It was high time I fetched Lorna away to the safety of our farm!

To the Rescue

I went home as fast as I could to tell my mother and sisters to get ready at once for visitors. Soon fires were blazing, the beds were aired and there was plenty of hot food.

I took our new light pony sled and roped myself to it like a horse, taking a wooden staff to help me along. My sister Annie had found a fur cloak to keep Lorna warm.

I left my sled at the top of the water slide, which was frozen hard, and reached Sir Ensor's house. I was not a moment too soon. Two of the Doone young men had broken in! Lorna was crouched behind a chair praying. Gwennie sprawled on the floor, gripping one of the men's ankles. I took hold of both of the rascals and pitched them through the window, head first into a snow drift.

Then I bundled the girls into the sled and we set off down the icy water slide between the black cliffs. Gwennie held Lorna safely in the sled with her strong chubby arms.

At last we arrived. My mother, Annie and Betty took Lorna and Gwennie to the fire and comforted them. They were soon all the best of friends. My mother kissed Lorna's forehead, as she lay sleeping at last, and said, 'God bless her, John!'

I fetched Gwennie a potful of bacon and peas and she ate the lot.

Lorna at Plovers' Barrow Farm

There was no fear the Doones would follow us, for, when the snow thawed, their valley was flooded. Also Jeremy Stickles and his troops kept watch on the Doones, who were the new King James's enemies.

Tom Faggus, who had got his pardon, came courting our Annie. He told Lorna her necklace was not glass at all, but diamonds, and worth a fortune. The ring she had given me had a family crest, and it turned out she was not Sir Ensor's grand-daughter at all. She was the little girl I had seen in the coach all those years ago, who had been kidnapped by the Doones. Her name was really Lady Lorna Dougal, and she was a great heiress.

All this made no difference to Lorna, who was happy to be safe in a real home at last. But when spring came at last, something happened to frighten her.

One day, as she was planting herbs in my mother's kitchen garden, the bushes parted and an evil face appeared. It was Carver Doone. With a deadly smile, he lifted his long gun and pointed it at her. Then he lowered it, and shot into the ground between her feet. She almost fainted with fright.

'Next time I will kill you,' snarled Carver, 'unless you come back tomorrow, bringing all you took away. And I will destroy that fool, John Ridd.'

No wonder the Doones wanted Lorna back. She was the heiress to the Earl of Lorne, their old enemy, who had lost them their lands.

Lorna said she wanted no money or title. All she wanted was to be my wife. So a day was set for the wedding, in our little village church. It would take place in the summer.

In spite of Carver's threats, our plans went on. Carver came one night with his men to set fire to the farm, but we were warned in time, and were waiting for him. I picked him up and threw him down in the farmyard muck, and shamed him in front of his men. He swore to be revenged on me.

But before that could happen, all the country folk made a determined attack on the Doone Valley to rescue one of their wives that the Doones had stolen. The Doones' village was burned, and Counsellor and Carver were the only ones to get away.

Carver had been seen galloping madly away on his black horse, but no one had heard of him since.

Blood on the Altar

That summer, folk came from miles around to see our wedding. The little church was so full I could hardly pick my way up the aisle for fear of treading on the women's gowns.

My darling Lorna looked so beautiful in her simple white dress I was almost afraid to look at her, until the ring had been put on her finger and we had both said, 'I will.'

Then she turned to look up at me lovingly with her clear brown eyes. The sound of a shot rang through the church, and the light in those eyes faded.

Lorna fell across my knees just as I was going to kiss her, and a flood of blood gushed out over the yellow altar step.

I lifted her up and called to her, but it was no good. The only sign of life was a drip of bright red blood.

Of course I knew who had done it. It could only be one devil – Carver Doone.

I laid my wife in my mother's arms and leaped on our best horse, with bridle but no saddle.

I do not know who pointed the way, but I took it, and all the men stood back.

I had no weapon of any sort and I knew he had a gun. In spite of that, I had no doubts that I would kill the man.

Far into the moors we raced, Carver in the lead. He thundered up the narrow passage towards Cloven Rocks. I knew his horse must slow down in that steep climb. To escape me, he took the fork at the crossroads that led to the treacherous bog called the Wizard's Marsh.

He had one hand on a pistol, but what cared I for pistols? A twisted old oak hung from the crag above me. Rising from my horse's back, I tore a great branch of it away from the trunk.

Carver Doone turned the corner suddenly, and came to the black, bottomless bog. With a start of fear, he wheeled his horse round, and came at me, but there was no way past.

His bullet struck me somewhere, but I took no notice. I laid my horse across his path and struck his steed with the oak branch. Man and horse rolled over.

Carver Doone was stunned for a moment. I leaped from my horse, and bared my arms as if for wrestling, kicking his pistol out of the way.

I think he knew, from my knotted muscles, the way I stood, and, most of all, from my stern blue eyes, that he had met his master. He was ashy pale, but he came at me with such a grip as I'd never felt before.

But my strength was like iron. I had him helpless in two minutes and his tongue lolled out. Then I flung him away from me.

'Carver Doone, thou art beaten! Own it and go thy way, repenting!'

It was too late. The black bog had him by the feet. We had not noticed how near we had come to it. He fell back, like a stumpy tree standing out of the marsh.

Then he tossed his arms to heaven. They were black to the elbow, and the glare in his eyes was ghastly. Joint by joint, he sank from sight, till there was nothing left but a dark brown bubble. The heavy bog was heaving and grinding its slimy jaws among the reeds.

I dragged myself up on my horse, and, in pain of mind and body, I rode home in a dream. The thought of Lorna's death was tolling like a funeral bell in my brain.

I was helped, staggering, to my bed, faint with the loss of blood from my wound, and lay unconscious for many days. At last a little of my strength came back and I opened my eyes. Lorna stood in the doorway!

Upsetting all the medicine bottles, and taking no notice of my thick bandages, she managed to get into my arms. Turning my pale face up, she kissed me.

It was not a moment to describe. I could not believe she had not died of the gunshot wound. The doctor was sent away and my former strength came back, with a darling wife and good food. As for Lorna, she never tired of sitting and watching me eat.

She never tires now of being with me. Year by year her beauty grows. And if I wish to tease her, by reminding her of past sadness, I only have to say two words.

'Lorna Doone.'